JF
Ind
vol.4

W9-AHE-566

INDIANA JONES™

AND THE
SPEAR OF DESTINY

PART FOUR

SCRIPT & COLORS
Elaine Lee

ART
Dan Spiegle

LETTERS
Carrie Spiegle

COVER ART
Hugh Fleming

DARK HORSE COMICS

Spotlight

VISIT US AT
www.abdopublishing.com

Reinforced library bound edition published in 2009 by Spotlight, a division of the ABDO Publishing Group, 8000 West 78th Street, Edina, Minnesota 55439. Spotlight produces high-quality reinforced library bound editions for schools and libraries. Published by agreement with Dark Horse Comics, Inc., and Lucasfilm Ltd.

Library of Congress Cataloging-in-Publication Data

Lee, Elaine.
 Indiana Jones and the Spear of Destiny / Elaine Lee, script, colors ; Will Simpson, pencils ; Dan Spiegle, inks ; Clem Robins, letters ; Hugh Fleming, cover art ; Teena Gores, publication design ; Bob Cooper & Dan Thorsland, edits. -- Reinforced library bound ed.
     p. cm. -- (Indiana Jones)
 "Dark Horse."
 ISBN 978-1-59961-580-6 (vol. 4)
 1. Graphic novels. [1. Graphic novels.] I. Simpson, Will, ill. II. Title.
 PZ7.7.L44In 2008
 [Fic]--dc22

                                                                    2008009794

All Spotlight books have reinforced library bindings and
are manufactured in the United States of America.

I WOULDN'T MOVE, IF I WERE YOU. I'VE GOT ONE OF YOUR BLUESHIRT BOYS, COLONEL...BUT I'D BE GLAD TO TRADE HIM FOR THE LADY.

HE'S NO BOY OF MINE...

...SO, YOU MAY KILL HIM IF YOU LIKE.

NOW, WAIT JUST A MOMENT!

THESE FELLAS ARE ALWAYS WILLIN' TO LAY DOWN THEIR LIVES FOR THE *CAUSE*, BUT I'LL NOT BE HAVIN' 'EM DIE FER A BLEEDIN' HISTORICAL ARTIFACT!

ROMANTIC OLD FOOL! I CARE NOTHING FOR YOUR CAUSE. IF WE HAD HAD THE CHOICE, WE WOULD HAVE HAD THE ENGLISH FOR OUR ALLIES.

SEE, CONNELY? NAZIS IN *THEORY* ARE ONE THING. NAZIS UP *CLOSE* ARE A WHOLE DIFFERENT BALL GAME!

KURT. HELP DR. JONES DOWN THE STAIRS.

"AND THE TWO SET THE CANDLES UPON THE TABLE, AND THE THIRD THE TOWEL UPON THE VESSEL, AND THE FOURTH THE *HOLY SPEAR* EVEN UPRIGHT UPON THE *VESSEL*.

"WITH THAT, THE KNIGHTS HEARD THE CHAMBER DOOR OPEN, AND THERE THEY SAW ANGELS; AND TWO BORE CANDLES OF WAX, AND THE THIRD A TOWEL, AND THE FOURTH A *SPEAR* WHICH *BLED MARVELOUSLY.*"

BOTH LEGENDS WITH MARVELOUS SPEARS, BOTH SPEARS CONNECTED TO MARVELOUS VESSELS...?

IT'S POSSIBLE, THAT IF YOUR IRISH SPEAR WERE TAKEN FROM IRELAND, INTO WALES...IT MAY HAVE TRAVELED OUT OF THE CELTIC WORLD TO JERUSALEM, VIA THE *ROMAN INVADERS*, SINCE ROME WAS OCCUPYING *BOTH* CELTIC BRITAIN AND THE HOLY LAND, JUST BEFORE THE TIME OF CHRIST.

...THE CAULDRON AND THE GRAIL!

AND ENDED UP IN TH' THIEVIN' HANDS OF A BLEEDIN' ROMAN *PIKER* NAME OF *LONGINUS!*

WHAT WAS IT THAT THE LADY IN THE CHAPEL SAID?

THE END